DENNIS the MENACE

A LICENCE TO MENACE!

BEANO**books**

published under licence by

meadowside
CHILDREN'S BOOKS

DENNIS THE DETECTIVE

It was just another boring day at Beanotown School.

Elastic bands whizzed across the hallways.

The school caretaker ducked and weaved as he made his way through the school, avoiding small missiles and pointed paper aeroplanes. Now and then he shook his fist at the classroom doors.

In the sick room the nurse was trying to deal with everything from nose bleeds to stink bomb allergies (not to mention paperclips in ears and one small boy with a strawberry up his left nostril). And most of her patients were there because of Dennis.

Dennis himself was even more bored than usual. He had tried to get out of the window but, after his exciting escape the previous week, all the classroom windows had been nailed shut. This was making everyone even more bad tempered than usual, because it was a hot day and there was no air. Everything smelled like stink bombs.

In the front row, all the softies were busily getting on with their work. At least, almost all the softies were. Walter and Spotty were starting on their Maths homework, but Bertie kept pausing in his algebra to stare into space.

Dennis let out a long sigh and absentmindedly aimed a paper aeroplane at the back of Walter's head. There was only one thing for it. He was going to have to make an escape plan. He glanced over at Curly and Pie Face. Curly was asleep and drooling on his Maths book. Pie Face was doodling pies all over his textbook. At Dennis's feet, Gnasher was gnawing on Walter the softy's favourite teddy. Dennis needed a distraction if he was going to escape, but it didn't look as if his menacing friends were gonna help him at all.

Just then Walter let out a loud wail.

"What's the matter, Walter dear?" asked Mr Hodges.

"My glasses are missing!" sobbed Walter. "I put them down for a moment to put some eye drops in my eyes and now they're gone!"

The classroom was in uproar. It was the perfect moment for Dennis to slip away. He winked at Gnasher and got ready to go and do a bit of menacing, when suddenly...

"DENNIS!" bellowed Mr Hodges. "Where are those glasses?"

Dennis folded his arms and scowled at Mr Hodges.

"I don't know!" Dennis growled. "What would I want with 'em?"

Mr Hodges clenched his fists and crumbled his piece of chalk into dust.

"I will not allow my favourite pupil to be upset!" he roared. "Where are those glasses, you menace?"

Before Dennis could reply, Gnasher sprang into action. He aimed at the seat of Mr Hodges's trousers and bit down hard.

"**YOWEE!**" shrieked Mr Hodges, clutching his bottom.

"Let's go, Gnasher!" called Dennis, and they raced out of the room before Mr Hodges could stop them.

Dennis and Gnasher raced down the corridor and skidded around the caretaker (who dropped his bucket of mop water for the fifteenth time that day). They shot out of the school and into the playground, where Mr Pump was taking a football lesson.

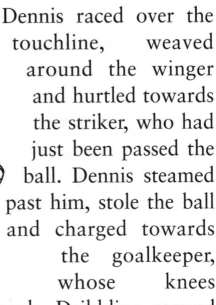

Dennis raced over the touchline, weaved around the winger and hurtled towards the striker, who had just been passed the ball. Dennis steamed past him, stole the ball and charged towards the goalkeeper, whose knees began to knock. Dribbling around three petrified defenders, Dennis flicked the ball into the air and, performing a perfect overhead scissor kick, he powered the ball straight past the goalkeeper's ear and slammed it into the back of the net.

As Mr Pump yelled **"GOAL!"** Dennis and Gnasher shot out of the school gates and disappeared up the road in a cloud of dust.

"Why would I take Walter's softy glasses?" Dennis raged to Gnasher when they were safely away from school. "I've done better menaces than that in my sleep!"

He started filling water bombs to throw at Minnie while he talked (there was no point in wasting menacing time).

"GNASH!" Gnasher agreed, wondering if it was time for tea yet.

"I can't let people think I'd do such a stupid menace!" Dennis went on. "There's only one thing for it. I'll have to find out who did take the stupid glasses! And that's gonna cut into my menacing time."

Just then, Minnie appeared at the corner and a grin spread slowly over Dennis's face. Three water bombs whizzed through the air and

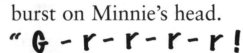

SPLAT! SPLAT! SPLAT!

burst on Minnie's head.
"G - r - r - r - r!
You - " she bellowed, pulling out a catapult. But Dennis had already gone!

10

Dennis raced home to his garage, which was packed to the roof with boxes full of old menacing equipment. Dennis rummaged around and found all sorts of old treasures... his very first catapult, his water-squirting dummy, his jet-propelled pushchair and even Gnasher's first dog basket, which was almost chewed to pieces.

At last, after emptying about half the boxes, Dennis found what he was looking for.

"My magnifying glass!" he grinned. He held it up and peered into the corner at an especially large spider. "This is gonna help me find clues," Dennis told Gnasher. He pocketed the spider (always the quickest way to cause a distraction) and sprinted out of the garage just as Mum walked in.

Mum was looking for her super-large pack of industrial-strength cleaner. Bea had found a tin of orange paint and redecorated the kitchen. But when she saw all the empty boxes, Mum staggered and forgot all about the orange paint. The entire garage was filled with menacing equipment she thought she would never have to see again.

Mum's mouth opened and closed silently. The car was completely buried under a mountain of water pistols. Old catapults dangled from the light and burst whoopee cushions fluttered in the air.

"Dennis!" said Mum through gritted teeth. Then she fainted backwards into a pile of Gnasher's old dog biscuits.

"I've gotta find some clues," Dennis told Gnasher as they raced into Beanotown. "Those glasses are hiding somewhere and I'm gonna find them! So I've gotta think like a detective – and what's the first thing that all detectives do?"

"Gnash?" asked Gnasher. He was hoping that whatever it was involved sausages.

"Return to the crime scene!" said Dennis. "Come on, let's go!"

They dashed up to the school just as the last teacher screeched out of the school gates in his car. Dennis examined every inch of the classroom through his magnifying glass. He emptied all the drawers, turned all the desks upside down, checked inside every cupboard and peered behind every shelf.

He found a couple of old water

pistols, six sweets covered in fluff, a love letter from Walter to his girlfriend Matilda (Dennis dropped it quickly and wiped his hands on his jumper in disgust) and five beetles living in Plug's old pencil case. Then, underneath Billy Whizz's chair, Dennis found his first proper clue. It was the cloth from inside a glasses case.

"Aha!" Dennis exclaimed, peering at the cloth through his magnifying glass. In the corner, e m b r o i d e r e d in pink thread, was the name 'Walter'. Next, Dennis glimpsed a pink ribbon on the floor under Minnie's desk. It was the ribbon Walter used to hang his glasses around his neck.

"Another clue!" Dennis said. "It's gotta be either Minnie or Billy!"

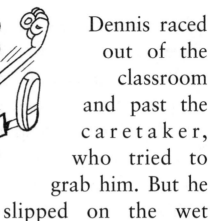

Dennis raced out of the classroom and past the c a r e t a k e r, who tried to grab him. But he slipped on the wet floor and landed with a BUMP in the mop bucket.

"Come back here!" he bellowed, trying to drag the bucket off his bottom and chase Dennis at the same time.

"Not likely!" chortled Dennis. He charged back out of school and down to the high street, just in time to see Minnie disappearing into the joke shop.

Dennis darted into the shop and hid behind a display of fake blood at the back of the shop. Minnie was looking through the scary masks and he watched her carefully. Her pockets had all sorts of bulges in them. Dennis could see a catapult-shaped bulge, a tennis-ball-shaped bulge and a mousetrap-shaped bulge, but no bulges that looked like glasses. If she had them, they must be in her rucksack.

As Minnie paid for a werewolf mask, Dennis got ready for a spot of menacing detective work. When Minnie walked out of the shop, Dennis made a flying leap through the air and grabbed her rucksack.

"OY!" screeched Minnie. "What are you playing at, Dennis?"

"You're the Great Beanotown Glasses Grabber!" Dennis bellowed, tugging the rucksack towards him.

"What would I want with that softy's glasses?"

Minnie roared, tugging the rucksack back towards her. Dennis held on to it so hard that the bag ripped in two, the contents flew into the air and Dennis and Minnie tumbled backwards. Dennis hit the fake blood display and Minnie crashed into the stink-bomb stand. Dennis looked at the contents of Minnie's bag as they zoomed over his head and hit the shopkeeper on the nose. The glasses weren't there! Dennis pulled a peg from his pocket, clipped it on his nose and burst out of the door with Minnie and Gnasher close behind him. Fake blood poured out of the door, over the step and onto the pavement.

"Help!" screamed Mrs Perkins (Spotty's mum), who was just passing the shop. She saw the fake blood and keeled over backwards.

"What's that stench?" squealed Gertrude Blenkinsop (Bertie's sister), clutching her nose and tripping over her high heels. Minnie glared at Dennis, her fists clenched. She had landed on a pile of the stink bombs and she smelled very bad indeed.

"This means I'm gonna have to take a bath!" Minnie fumed. "And I've already had one this month!"

"Want to borrow a peg?" asked Dennis with a grin.

"Come back here!" bellowed the shopkeeper.

"OY! You!" shouted a familiar voice. Sergeant Slipper was pounding up the road towards them. Dennis sprang to his feet and Gnasher gave himself a good shake, spraying fake blood in all directions.

Then Dennis grabbed
his skateboard and
whizzed around
the corner before
Sergeant Slipper
had chance
to blink.

Dennis headed over to Billy's house. The glasses cloth had been under Billy's chair – he must have the glasses. But Billy was not going to be as easy to catch as Minnie.

"We've gotta think of a plan to trap him," Dennis told Gnasher. They stopped outside Billy's house and Dennis drew a roll of tennis net from his back pocket.

"I knew this would come in useful!" he grinned. He strung the net across Billy's front door and rang the doorbell. It opened at once and a figure shot out, got tangled in the net and landed in a heap at Dennis's feet. Dennis whipped out his water pistol and blasted them with jets of water.

"**ARRGGHH!**" roared the captive, struggling to stand up. It wasn't Billy – it was his Mum – going out for her afternoon jog!

"Where's Billy?" fumed Dennis.

At that moment a blur whizzed past them in a cloud of dust.

"**GNASHER!**" yelled Dennis,

jumping on his skateboard. Gnasher leaped out from behind a bush as Billy zoomed down the path, skidded between his legs and tripped him up.

CRASH!

Dennis powered over Billy and Gnasher and screeched to a stop. He jumped off his skateboard, grabbed Billy and held on tight.

"Where are they?" he growled.

"Where are what?" asked Billy. "And why did you squirt my mum with a water pistol?"

"If I don't find that softy's glasses, I'm gonna be accused of a completely stupid menace!" Dennis raged. "You're my number-one suspect and I'm not gonna let the whole of Beanotown think I took them!"

"Well I didn't take them!" said Billy. "What would I want with them? If I wore glasses they'd have to be made of super-strong material to cope with my speed!"

"Turn out your pockets!" Dennis ordered.

Billy shoved his hands in his pockets and pulled out a yoyo, a ball of string, a couple of melted chocolate mini eggs left over from

Easter and a small dormouse. But there were no glasses.

"You were my only suspect," groaned Dennis. "If you don't have them, who does?"

"Not my problem!" grinned Billy, shaking himself free of Dennis's grip. He zoomed off into the distance. Dennis frowned so hard his eyebrows knitted together.

"This is turning into a bad day," he told Gnasher. "I haven't had time to do any menacing at all."

"GNASH!" agreed Gnasher. It had been a bad day for sausages as well.

Just then they saw someone walking slowly along on the other side of the road, feeling their way and using the garden walls as a guide.

"There's just one more suspect to try," said Dennis as a menacing gleam shone in his eyes. "Walter the softy himself!"

Gnasher looked doubtful.

"It's a long shot," said Dennis. "But we might pick up a few more clues… and have a bit of fun along the way!"

Dennis and Gnasher followed Walter along the street to Matilda's house. Walter knocked on the door and Matilda answered it.

"Oh, Matilda-wilda," said Walter with a softy blush. "I picked you some flowers. They're almost as pretty as you!"

"Oh!" simpered Matilda in delight. Then her smile changed to a scowl. "What are those? You think I look like a weed?!"

Walter was holding a bunch of ragged nettles and dandelions!

"Oh, if only I had my glasses!" Walter wailed.

Dennis snorted with laughter as Matilda slammed the door in Walter's face.

Walter walked on down the street, unaware that Dennis was close behind him.

Dennis could see someone coming towards Walter. They were walking in a very strange way – weaving and swerving all over the pavement, just like Walter.

"Has someone else had their glasses grabbed?" wondered Dennis. But then he saw that it was Bertie Blenkinsop, and he was wearing a big pair of glasses.

Walter blundered sideways, bumped into a dustbin and apologised to it. Bertie put his arms out in front of him, clutched at a tree and tried to shake hands with it.

"Hmmm," said Dennis. "Come to think of it, I've never seen Bertie wearing glasses before!"

At that moment, SMACK! Bertie and Walter walked into each other and fell down, clutching their noses and wailing.

Dennis strode over to them. He grabbed the glasses from Bertie's face and shoved them on Walter's nose. Walter stopped sobbing, peered through them and squealed in excitement.

"My glasses! My lovely glasses!"

Dennis could hardly believe it. Had Bertie gone potty?

"Are you trying to turn into a menace?" Dennis asked Bertie in amazement.

29

"No!" sobbed Bertie. "But I want to be like Walter so much! When I saw his glasses lying on the table, I couldn't resist! I thought he had a spare pair! I threw the ribbon and the cloth away – I'm sorry, Walter!"

"Oh Bertie," gushed Walter, "I quite understand! Of course you would want to look like me!"

"UGGHH! Stop it!" roared Dennis. He was starting to feel sick. "I've missed out on a whole day's menacing just to prove I didn't take Walter's softy glasses! You're gonna tell everyone in school that you took them!"

"Oh, I can't!" sobbed Bertie, his knees quivering. "Mr Hodges will tell me off! He might give me detention! I couldn't bear the shame!"

"It's all right, Bertie," said Walter

pompously. "Dennis can take the blame... he's used to it."

"Oh yeah?" growled Dennis. He pushed his face up so close to Walter's that their noses were almost touching. The sweet, perfumed smell of Walter made Dennis's nose twitch in horror.

"If I keep quiet about Bertie grabbing your glasses, after all the menacing time I lost today, I want something in return!"

"Wh... what do you want?" asked Walter, his knees trembling.

"An ice cream a day for a month," said Dennis. "And a big juicy bone for Gnasher every other day!"

"Anything to save Bertie from the shame of detention!" cried Walter. "Who can blame him for wanting to be more like me?"

"Mental," said Dennis to Gnasher.

"Oh Walter, you're my hero!" sighed Bertie.

"Look!" cried Walter, pointing over Dennis's shoulder. Dennis turned around and a grin spread wide across his face.

A huge crowd of people was marching towards him. Minnie was leading the charge, still ponging slightly (even after three baths). The school caretaker was there, still trying to tug the mop bucket off his bottom. The entire school football team was there too, together with Dennis's mum, the joke-shop owner, Mrs Perkins, Gertie Blenkinsop, Sergeant Slipper and Billy's mum.

"Er, maybe it hasn't been such a bad day for menacing after all!" chortled Dennis, leaping onto his skateboard. "Come on, Gnasher. **SCARPER!**"

MENACE MAN

"Mighty Man is way better than Amazing Man," Curly said, peering over at Pie Face's comic. "Only rubbish superheroes wear capes."

"At least Amazing Man doesn't wear his underpants over his trousers," retorted Pie Face, jabbing a finger at Mighty Man's blue and yellow outfit.

Dennis, Pie Face and Curly were sitting on the bridge reading their comics (in between dropping water bombs on the heads of passers by). Dennis elbowed both of them.

"Shut up!" he said.

"Here comes the Colonel!"

They waited until the Colonel was in position and then dropped three water bombs on him, one after the other.

"Who? What? Where?" spluttered the Colonel. But he could not see the menaces, so he stomped on his way, wringing out his hat and muttering.

"Amazing Man has got a stupid fatal weakness," continued Curly, flicking through his comic. "He's got really bad hay fever – that's daft!"

"Yeah, but at least Amazing Man works alone – he doesn't need a wet sidekick like Mighty Man does!" Pie Face argued.

"Shut UP!" grumbled Dennis again. "I'm sick of hearing about those stupid superheroes – and here comes that sap Bertie Blenkinsop!"

The three menaces took careful aim.

WHACK! OOOF! SPLASH!

Their water bombs got Bertie's head, stomach and shoes at the same time. Dennis roared with laughter as Bertie ran home wailing.

"Mighty Man's arch enemy is way cooler

than Amazing Man's arch enemy," Curly went on. Dennis rolled his eyes.

"What do you reckon, Dennis?" asked Pie Face. "Who's the best superhero – Amazing Man or Mighty Man?"

"Huh," said Dennis. "Your softy superheroes are just like Walter in a pair of tights! They're both rubbish!"

"Oh yeah?" said Pie Face. "So which superhero do you think is best?"

"None of them," said Dennis. "A real superhero would be a menacing mastermind who would really scare off the bad guys and show them who was boss!"

"Stop arguing," said Curly suddenly. "Here comes Spotty Perkins – get your water bombs ready!"

When they had run out of water bombs they headed for the skate park to practise their softy-squashing techniques. But all the talk about superheroes had given Dennis an idea.

"You know what Beanotown is missing?" he asked Gnasher as he performed an ollie over the heads of three snivelling softies. "A real baddy-bashing superhero! And I know just the menace for the job!"

"Gnash?" asked Gnasher hopefully. He could see it already – Super-Gnasher! Terror of pampered poodles everywhere!

"No, me!" Dennis exclaimed. "You can be my trusty sidekick! We'll rid Beanotown of everyone who causes trouble – for us!"

Dennis raced home and to Mum's wardrobe. He was sure he had seen just the thing he was looking for in there. He searched through piles of nylon nighties and viscose vests until he found it – a red and black striped cape that Mum had worn for Hallowe'en one year. (She had dressed up as Dennis and scared all the neighbours silly.)

Dennis cut the main part of the cape off until it was just long enough for Gnasher. Then he fastened it around Gnasher's neck. Next, Dennis cut a long, thin strip of material and snipped two eyes holes into it. Then he tied it around his head and grinned at Gnasher. "Menace Man and Danger Dog!" he chortled. "Beanotown's not gonna know what hit it!"

Menace Man pulled out a piece of paper and made a list of arch enemies. It was quite long.

"Humph," said Menace Man. "There's a lot of arch enemies to conquer. Maybe I'll just take the top five today

WALTER
the COLONEL
Sgt SLIPPER
BERTIE
SPOTTY
MINNIE

– we can start on the rest tomorrow."

Dennis loaded up his pockets with superhero equipment, grabbed his Menacemobile and headed for the Beanotown police station, where arch-enemy number one was just creeping up on a couple of unsuspecting menaces.

Sergeant Slipper had been having a very good day. He had told nine boys off for playing football too loudly. He had written a long report for the chief constable about why he should be given more holiday time. He had confiscated a yoyo and a catapult from Curly, and he was planning to play with them later. Best of all, he hadn't seen Dennis all day.

And now he was going to catch two menaces! The boys were hiding behind a hedge with peashooters, waiting for Billy to whizz past so they could get in some moving-target practice. Sergeant Slipper crept up behind them, his arms raised ready to catch them.

Closer! Closer...

POW! A custard bomb hit the back of his head and he spun around. **SPLAT!** Another custard bomb hit him in the face.

"Run, menaces!" yelled Dennis. "I'll take care of him!"

"It's Menace Man!" yelled the menaces as they ran in the opposite direction. **"WICKED!"**

"Who did that?" bellowed Sergeant Slipper, wiping globs of custard out of his eyes. When he spotted Dennis his mouth opened very wide – just wide enough for Dennis to aim a third custard bomb into it.

"UMPHUMMBURBLE!" spluttered the amazed Sergeant Slipper.

"I'm here to make sure you leave all menaces alone!" yelled Dennis. "And Danger Dog is here to make sure you learn how to keep fit!

Dennis chuckled as Gnasher sped towards Sergeant Slipper, his cape flying out behind him. Sergeant Slipper turned and ran as fast as he could back to his comfy police station!

"That's dealt with arch enemy number one," Dennis said, brushing his hands. "Now for arch enemy number two!"

The Colonel was doing what he enjoyed best; he was shouting.

"Outrageous!" he bawled. "Your commanding officer will hear about this!"

Bea, who he was shouting at, blew an enormous raspberry.

"Unbelievable!" hollered the Colonel. "First you crawl through my training grounds and leave sticky handprints all over my best soldiers, and now you blow raspberries at me! Intolerable! We're going to see your parents!"

The Colonel picked Bea up by her nappy. She squirmed and struggled, but she couldn't quite get free. Just then...

KERPOW! A stink bomb burst at the Colonel's feet.

PWANG! A dried pea shot the pin that held Bea's nappy and opened it. Bea dropped to the ground and started to crawl away, but stopped

45

in amazement when she saw who held the peashooter.

"Scarper Bea!" cried Menace Man. "He's not going anywhere!"

Bea darted through a hole in the garden fence and escaped. Dennis clasped a peg onto his nose as the Colonel pointed at him in astonishment.

"Who...?

What...?"

But the combination of the stink bomb and Bea's nappy was too much for him – he went green and keeled over backwards.

"Germ warfare!" he gasped as he fainted.

Walter the softy was having a doll's tea party with his two dearest chums, Bertie and Spotty.

"More tea, Fluffy Bunny?" asked

Spotty, pouring out a cup of watery tea for his favourite soft toy.

"Would you like a butterfly cake, Jemima?" Bertie asked his little doll.

"Who would like to sing a happy song about flowers with me?" simpered Walter.

The three softies had just started to sing when **SMASH!** A stink bomb landed in the middle of their tea party table!

"Hold it!" bellowed a menacing voice. "No softy singing allowed!"

Dennis dropped down from the tree where he had been hiding and Gnasher landed beside him, his cape acting as a parachute.

"Save me!" wailed Spotty, diving under the table. The dolls and teddies were flung into the bushes around them.

E-E-E-E-E-EEK! screeched Bertie, throwing the teapot into the air in terror. Walter tried to catch it but he missed and it landed on his foot.

"WAHH-H!" cried Walter, hopping around and clutching his throbbing toe.

"Menace Man is here to save the day!" Dennis declared. "The streets of Beanotown will be free from softy tea parties!"

"The smell!" wailed Walter. "I can't bear the smell!"

The three softies fled, holding their noses and calling for their mumsies. Gnasher quickly dug a hole, then buried all the dolls and teddies. Dennis helped him flatten down the earth.

"A good day's work, Danger Dog!" said Menace Man. "We've conquered our first five arch-enemies! This calls for a sausage feast!"

Dennis and Gnasher raced towards the butcher's shop, but suddenly Dennis was running alone. He swirled around and glowered through his red-and-black mask. Someone had caught Gnasher by his cape. It was Dad!

"You can't capture a superhero!" Dennis growled.

"Every superhero has an evil rival!" said Dad. "I've been hearing all sorts of stories about a masked menace! You're coming home and going to your room!"

"You can't send a superhero to his room!" fumed Dennis.

"Your sidekick is now in my power! You have no choice!"

Dad held the struggling Gnasher in a tight grip and marched off. Dennis followed him back home and saw Mum in the doorway with her arms folded.

"So that's where my cape went!" she exclaimed when she saw Gnasher and Dennis. "I've had to spend all morning tidying up my wardrobe!"

"Right," said Dad, heading upstairs. "Gnasher's going to be locked in your room!"

"Where Danger Dog goes, I go!" Dennis growled, stomping up the stairs behind Dad. Soon they were stuck in the bedroom.

"TRAPPED!" said Dennis. "But that doesn't mean they've won. You can't keep a menacing superhero down!"

Dennis opened his wardrobe and a pile of menacing equipment fell out.

"My emergency stash!" Dennis grinned, opening the window. Soon the windowsill was bristling with catapults, rubber arrows, peashooters and lots of water-bomb launchers.

"Now all I need is an arch enemy!" Dennis told Gnasher. He didn't have to wait long.

Minnie was caught in a hail of small missiles – Dennis used one peashooter while he reloaded another with lightning speed.

Billy slipped on a banana skin that Dennis catapulted onto the path ahead of him.

Walter's girlfriend Matilda had her new hairstyle ruined by a carefully aimed paintball.

Dennis was just refreshing his stink bomb supply, ready for the next passer by, when he noticed something unusual. Over at the Colonel's house, someone was climbing out of a window – and it wasn't the Colonel. Dennis grabbed his binoculars and trained them on the man. He was carrying a large sack and his pockets were bulging. Dennis could just see a glint of gold. He focused his binoculars on the pockets. Then he grabbed his bow and rubber arrows.

"This is a job for Menace Man!" he roared. He took aim, fired and… THUNK! The rubber arrow landed right in the middle of the burglar's forehead! The shock made him lose his balance and he toppled out of the window into the Colonel's begonias.

"Come on, Danger Dog!" Dennis

yelled. He climbed onto the windowsill and shimmied down the drainpipe, while Gnasher again used his cape as a parachute and floated down to the ground. They raced over to where the burglar was just crawling out of the begonias, with leaves sticking out of his ears.

"Gotcha!" Dennis yelled. He sprang into the air and landed on top of the burglar.

"O-O-O-OF!" gasped the burglar as Dennis flattened him. The sack fell open to reveal all the Colonel's favourite toy soldiers. But Dennis was looking at the gold coins pouring out of the burglar's pockets.

"Danger Dog, you know what to do!" he ordered.

Gnasher raced off and returned after a few minutes, dragging Sergeant Slipper by the ankles of his trousers. When Sergeant Slipper saw the burglar, he got very excited.

"You're going behind bars!" he roared.

"Anything!" gasped the burglar. "Anything! Just get this menace off me!"

"Splendid show, old boy!" exclaimed the Colonel when he found his toy soldiers were safe. "Deserve a medal!"

"The local paper wants to interview you!" gasped Mum in delight. "My son the hero!"

"Not bad, not bad at all," agreed Dad.

Bea just blew an enormous raspberry.

Dennis and Gnasher went to meet Curly and Pie Face in the skate park.

"Never thought I'd see you as the local hero," sniggered Curly.

"Didn't think you cared about the Colonel's soldiers that much," added Pie Face with a smirk.

"I don't care about his soldiers," snorted Dennis. "But I do care about his health!"

"Eh?" asked Curly and Pie Face.

"The burglar's pockets were full of gold!" Dennis grinned. He emptied his pockets and piled gold coins onto his skateboard. "Chocolate gold!"

"Wicked!" gasped Pie Face, letting the chocolate coins run through his fingers.

"We all know that chocolate's bad for grown ups," Dennis chortled. "So I thought we should help the Colonel out!"

There was a flurry of hands and elbows, and a few minutes later the three menaces were surrounded by nothing more than piles of screwed-up gold paper. Pie Face gave a loud burp. "MMM! Chocolate – almost as delicious as pies!" he enthused.

"You know, Amazing Man's OK," said Curly, curling his hands over his chocolate-filled stomach.

"Yeah, and Mighty Man's all right," added Pie Face. "But we all know who the best, most menacing superhero really is!"

MENACE MAN

THE DAD FILES

Dennis was silent.

Curly and Pie Face were silent.

Even Gnasher was silent.

It was Pie Face's birthday, and he had just opened the most amazing present he had ever seen.

"Awesome," gasped Curly at last.

A slow grin was just starting to spread over Dennis's face.

"A secret agent kit!" he chuckled. "You know what this means? We've been given a licence to menace!"

There was a flurry of arms, legs and heavy boots as they all dived for the kit. Inside was a treasure trove of secret-agent gadgets – binoculars, skeleton keys, rope ladders, bugging devices, a miniature camera, not to mention a water-squirting watch and three walkie talkies.

Soon the gadgets were divided between the three menaces.

"Who's it from?" asked Dennis.

"My cousin," Pie Face explained. "He told me to open it away from Mum."

Dennis took a small black pad and a stubby pencil from his back pocket, licked the pencil and wrote MISSION 1 at the top of the page. Then he stopped.

"So what's the first mission?" asked Curly.

Dennis chucked two of the walkie talkies at Curly and Pie Face, then turned the third on.

"Stay in contact," he told them. "As soon as we get our first mission I'll let you know. Right now I've got a bit of work to do on my skateboard."

Dennis jumped onto his board and zoomed down the street, grinding along the kerb and making Mrs Perkins drop her shopping.

"Come back here, you menace!"

she yelled, shaking her fist so hard that her wig slipped to one side. But Dennis just whizzed around the corner and jumped over the gate into his back garden. He went straight into the shed and closed the door.

For the next hour there were some very peculiar sounds and smells coming out of that shed.

There were bangs and burps.

There were puffs of smoke and gloopy gurgles.

At last the shed door opened and Dennis came out with Gnasher at his side.

Dennis had his skateboard under one arm, a blob of oil on his nose and a very familiar gleam in his eyes. The shed was still gently smoking as he marched up to the house and let himself in at the back door.

Dennis peered through the kitchen door and saw Dad standing in the hallway, talking to someone on the phone.

"I have to keep my voice down," Dad was saying. "I just want to confirm the time. Seven o'clock – and make sure everything's ready!"

Dennis's eyes narrowed as Dad put the phone down. Gnasher frowned and looked up at Dennis.

"So, Dad's plotting something, is he?" mused Dennis. "No one's gonna keep a secret from me and my spies! Come on, Gnasher, we're on the case!"

Dennis raced out into the garden and pressed the button on his walkie talkie.

"Come in, agents! Can you hear me?"

"Loud and clear, chief!" crackled Curly's voice.

"We've got our first mission!"

Dennis, Curly and Pie Face met in one of their dens in Beanotown Park.

Dennis told them all about Dad's mysterious phone call.

"He's up to something," Dennis finished. "And we're gonna find out what it is!"

"Brilliant!" said Pie Face.

"From now on, where Dad goes, we go," Dennis went on. "We've gotta stay out of sight and shadow him!"

"What are we waiting for?"" bellowed Curly. "Let's go!"

They raced back to Dennis's house, just in time to see Dad walking down the garden path and carrying a large bag. Dennis stopped so suddenly that Curly and Pie Face bumped into him with a loud

SCRUNCH!

"OW! By doze!" groaned Pie Face.

"Shh!" hissed Dennis as Dad turned around. They ducked behind a hedge until he started walking again.

Walter's mumsy was tripping along the pavement towards Dad. Dennis grinned, waiting for Dad to cross the road to avoid her as usual. But then Dennis's mouth dropped open. Dad was hurrying up to her! He was stopping to talk to her!

"What's wrong with him?" gasped Dennis. "He can't stand Walter's mumsy! He always pretends to be asleep when she comes to gossip with Mum!"

Walter's mumsy was giggling. Then she nodded her head and made the pink fluffy flower on her hat wobble.

"Maybe he's asking for tips on how to turn you into a softy," Pie Face suggested. Dennis punched him in the arm.

"Maybe he's asking her if she'd like to adopt you!" grinned Curly.

"Har har," said Dennis with a smirk. "Maybe he's asking her to send Walter over to play at your houses!"

That wiped the grins off their faces.

Dad said goodbye to Walter's mumsy and carried on walking towards the shops.

"Have you got the binoculars?" asked Dennis. Pie Face pulled the binoculars out of his pocket and handed them to Dennis, who clapped them to his eyes. He was just in time to see Dad disappearing into the dry cleaners. Dennis, Curly and Pie Face scooted into the dairy opposite and peered out of the window.

"Very weird," muttered Dennis. Dad never ever went into the dry cleaners. In fact, Mum had said just the other day that she was still waiting for Dad to clean the suit he got married in.

Dennis looked through the binoculars, but all he could see was the bald patch on Dad's head.

He took a couple of pictures with his tiny secret-agent camera.

"What's he doing now?" asked Curly, trying to look through the binoculars. Dennis elbowed him out of the way and Curly trod on the dairy owner's in-growing toenail.

"**YOWEEEEEEE!** What are you troublemakers up to?" he bellowed. "Go on, get out. I know your dads!"

"Lucky him!" grinned Pie Face as they darted out of the door. "Look – your Dad's on the move again!"

Dad had left the dry cleaners and was strolling down to the end of the street, whistling.

"He never whistles!" Dennis frowned. "There's something very fishy going on here. "Why is he so cheerful?"

"Maybe he's sending you to boarding school," said Curly.

"Yeah, right!" Dennis guffawed. "Like there's any boarding school in the country that would hold me!"

"Maybe he's going away to boarding school, and he took his old school uniform to the dry cleaners?" said Pie Face.

"Nah," Dennis replied. "He's way too ancient. Besides, you can't teach an old dog new tricks."

"GNASH!" agreed Gnasher.

"Hold it!" Dennis exclaimed, stopping suddenly. "He's gone into… I don't believe it!" He rubbed his eyes and shook the binoculars. "He's gone into the flower shop!"

"Urrgh," cried Pie Face.

"Yuck!" Curly grimaced.

"This calls for serious secret-agent action," said Dennis. He looked up at the roof of the flower shop. There was a window cleaner's ladder leaning against the shop next door.

"Come on!" cried Dennis. He grabbed the ladder and raced over to the flower shop.

"OY!"

roared the window cleaner, who had been up the ladder. He was now clinging to the windowsill with his fingers. "You bring that ladder back here now! Help!"

"I'm just borrowing it!" Dennis replied as he leaned the ladder against

the flower shop wall. "Come on, we've gotta hear what Dad's saying!"

Dennis, Curly and Pie Face dashed up the ladder and onto the roof, while Gnasher stayed on the ground to keep a lookout.

"Bark if there's danger!" Dennis told Gnasher. "Pie Face, where's that rope?"

Dennis tied one end of the rope around his waist and handed the other end to Curly and Pie Face.

75

Then he opened
the skylight and
peered down into
the shop. He could
see the top of Dad's
head and the
flower-shop
owner's curly red
perm, but he
couldn't hear what
they were saying.

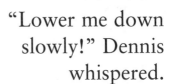

"Lower me down
slowly!" Dennis
whispered.

Pie Face and Curly
took the strain and started to lower
Dennis down on the rope.

Dennis spread his arms and legs
out wide to get his balance, and
strained his ears to hear what Dad

was saying. He waved at Curly to lower him further.

On the roof, Curly and Pie Face were pink in the face. Beads of sweat were popping out all over their foreheads.

"A bit more!" puffed Curly. "Just a bit further!"

Inside, Dennis was getting closer and closer to the top of Dad's head. He snapped a couple more pictures of the bald spot. Dad nodded.

"That's all arranged then," he said. "But keep it quiet!"

Just then a pie van rumbled along the street past the flower shop. A wonderful aroma of hot pies wafted up to the roof and hovered under Pie Face's nose.

Pie Face's nose twitched.

It quivered.

Then it turned to follow the smell – and the rest of Pie Face turned too!

"Pie Face, I can't hold the rope myself!" bellowed Curly as the rope slithered through his hands.

"CRASH!" Dennis dropped like a stone, but luckily his fall was broken by the flower arranging table.

"WHOOSH!" Flowers of every size, shape and colour were catapulted into the air.

SNAP! The table cracked down the middle.

TING! The door tinkled as Dad left, unaware of what was happening behind him.

Dennis jumped to his feet and faced the flower shop owner. She had her hands on her hips and a plant pot upside down on her head.

"What do you think—"

Dennis darted out of the door and looked up and down the street, but Dad had vanished. Curly scrambled down the ladder and passed Dennis his skateboard.

Pie Face was disappearing into the distance behind the pie van.

"Did you see where Dad went?" Dennis said. "We've gotta follow him!"

"Oho, no you don't, you young rascal!" trumpeted a loud voice. Dennis and Curly turned to see the navy blue chest of Sergeant Slipper. "You're coming to the station with me to explain this flower fiasco!"

By now flowers were whirling all around the street and plant pots were rolling in the gutters.

"SCARPER!" yelled Curly and Dennis. Curly sped off in one direction while Dennis leapt onto his skateboard and made off up the high street.

"You don't get away that easily!" roared Sergeant Slipper. He jumped on his bicycle and gave chase.

Dennis just grinned and kicked a button on his skateboard. A jet of oil squirted out from the back of his board. Sergeant Slipper wobbled all over the road as his bicycle wheels skidded on the slick. With a loud yell he fell bottom-first into a puddle of oil.

"I'll get you, you menace!" Sergeant Slipper shouted, shaking his fist.

"You've gotta catch me first!" chortled Dennis. He kicked another button on his board and there was a roar of flames as his jet-propelled engine fired up.

"Every secret agent needs a getaway vehicle!" he chuckled to Gnasher as they sped away.

But as Dennis screeched around a corner he hit his neighbour the Colonel's toy soldiers, who were out on parade. The soldiers shot into the air like tiny rockets and **WALLOP!** One of them hit the Colonel in the eye.

"Insubordination!" Revolution!" The Colonel hollered, grabbing the soldier as his eye started to swell. "It's the firing squad for you, my lad!"

"Quick, Colonel, have you seen my dad?" Dennis asked. But the

Colonel grasped Dennis's collar and his eyes popped out of their sockets.

"Your dad? Oh yes, I'll be seeing your dad all right! He'll be paying for a brand new regiment!"

Dennis struggled but the Colonel had him in an iron grip. Then he remembered the secret agent watch. It had been made to squirt water, but Dennis had made a few modifications to that, too…

"**AAARGH!** the Colonel shouted as he got an eyeful of cold custard.

"We're under attack! RETREAT! RETREAT!"

He let go of Dennis's collar and Dennis zoomed off at top speed, crunching more soldiers under his wheels as he went.

When Dennis got home, he tiptoed through the hall, past Bea (who was ripping the heads off her newest dolls) and over to the telephone. Working fast, he pulled the phone-bugging device from one pocket and an old piece of chewing gum from the other.

He quickly stuck the bug to the phone with the chewing gum. Then he went through the photos he had taken that day. Walter's mumsy, the dry cleaners, the flower shop... it was all very suspicious. And Dennis still had no idea what Dad was up to.

Dennis raced out to the garden and took up position behind the shed. Now all he had to do was wait for the phone to ring.

BRRRR! BRRRR!

Dennis clamped the listening device to his ear. But it wasn't Dad who answered the phone. It was Mum!

"Hello?" she said. Then she screamed. "YUCK! What's this on the phone? UGH! It's chewing gum! It's gone into my ear! DENNIS!"

Dennis darted out from behind the shed, but for once Dad had moved like lightning! He grabbed Dennis by the scruff of his neck and dragged him into the house. Mum was standing in the middle of the kitchen with the phone receiver chewing gummed to her ear.

"Get this off me!" she bellowed.

"Dennis, go to your room," said Dad. "And..."

(Dennis thought he knew what was coming.)

"... and change into your best clothes," finished Dad.

"Why?" Dennis demanded in amazement

"Never you mind!" said Dad. "Just do it!"

Dennis stomped upstairs and slammed his bedroom door shut. If he had to wear his best clothes, that meant just one thing. A party. And judging by Dad's eccentric behaviour, he was gonna be inviting Walter's mumsy, which meant...

"Walter the softy's gonna be there!" choked Dennis in horror.

He pulled open his backpack and grabbed the rope ladder.

"No way am I getting into some stupid clothes and going to a party with Walter the softy," Dennis told Gnasher. He attached the ladder to the window ledge and unrolled it. "Sorry Gnasher, you can't climb down this ladder. I'll come and rescue you later when they've gone to the party."

"GNASH!" nodded Gnasher. Dennis sped down the rope ladder and darted off to find Curly and Pie Face.

It took Dennis a long time to find his secret agents. He tried the skate park, but they weren't there. He tried the high street and had to duck down an alleyway to escape Sergeant Slipper. He tried the toyshop, but only the Colonel was in there. (Dennis created a distraction by toppling a display of crying dolls over.) He even tried the pie shop, but there was no sign of them. Finally he remembered the walkie talkies, pushed the button and spoke into it.

"Curly! Pie Face! Can you hear me?"

"Loud and clear!" crackled Pie Face's voice. "Er, Dennis—"

"We've got a rescue mission!" Dennis interrupted. "Gnasher's stuck in my bedroom at home and we've gotta get him out!"

"DENNIS!" bellowed Curly and Pie Face together.

"OY!" roared Dennis, rubbing his ear.

"Gnasher's not at your house!" said Pie Face. "You'd better come and meet us. We're outside the Hairless Cat. Hurry!"

Dennis jumped on his skateboard. The Hairless Cat was the most expensive restaurant in town. It had just been opened by Gregory Ripples, the celebrity chef, and it was so exclusive that hardly anyone could afford to go there. What were Curly and Pie Face doing there?

Dennis screeched to a halt when he saw his friends outside the twinkling lights of the Hairless Cat. They were alone.

"So – where's Gnasher?" he asked.

Pie Face and Curly just pointed. As Dennis followed their fingers his mouth fell open. Sitting around a table in the window of the Hairless Cat were Mum, Dad, Bea… and Gnasher!

"I chased that pie van all over Beanotown," Pie Face explained. "Its last delivery was here – and that's when I saw them!"

"We managed to put a bugging device on Bea's dummy," added Curly, handing the listening device to Dennis.

Dennis put the listener in his ear and over the sound of Bea sucking her dummy, he heard Dad say, "Happy anniversary, Mum!"

"I can't believe you arranged all this! Mum simpered. "Such beautiful flowers – and you got your suit cleaned!"

"I asked Walter's mumsy for advice about a present," added Dad.

"I love my new earrings!" Mum giggled.

"Oh no," Dennis groaned. "It was all for their anniversary. I've wasted all that menacing time and missed a slap-up feed!"

"I dunno about missing out on menacing," said Pie Face. "There was the window cleaner, the flower shop..."

"...Sergeant Slipper..." added Curly.

"... and the Colonel," agreed Dennis. "I guess secret agents are really just menaces in disguise!"

Suddenly there was a loud bark and Dennis looked down. Gnasher was standing at his feet, and in his jaws was...

"A Hairless-Cat doggy bag – from my hairy doggy!" yelled Dennis.

"Awesome!" grinned Pie Face

And the three secret agents tucked in to their own slap-up meal!

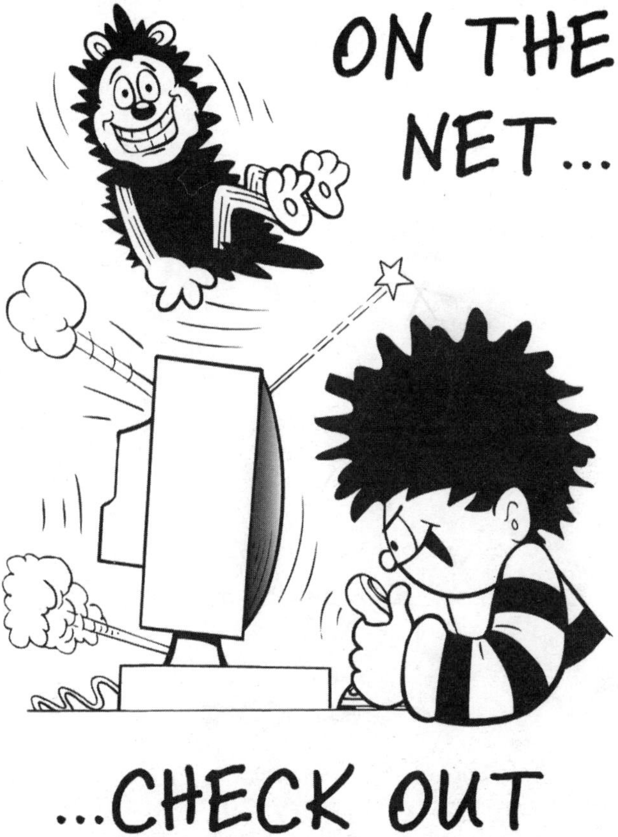

Written by RACHEL ELLIOT

Illustrated by BARRIE APPLEBY

published under licence by

CHILDREN'S BOOKS

185 Fleet Street, London, EC4A 2HS

"The Beano" ®©, "Dennis the Menace" ®©
and "Gnasher" ®© D.C. Thomson & Co., Ltd., 2006
Printed and bound in Great Britain by William Clowes Ltd, Beccles, Suffolk